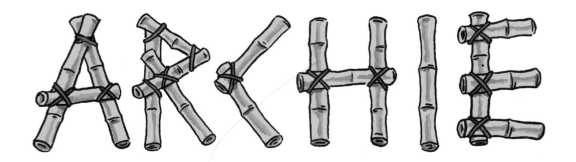

ARCHIE

and the Pirates

By Marc Rosenthal

JOANNA COTLER BOOKS
An Imprint of HarperCollinsPublishers

Archie and the Pirates
Copyright © 2009 by Marc Rosenthal
Manufactured in China.

Library of Congress Cataloging-in-Publication Data is available.
ISBN 978-0-06-144164-6

Typography by Carla Weise
09 10 11 12 13 LEO 10 9 8 7 6 5 4 3 2 1
❖
First Edition

For my mom,
who loved everything I ever did
—M.R.

After a night dreaming of drifting and floating · · ·

. . . Archie awakes to find
himself on a strange beach.

He does not know where
he is, *and* he is starting
to get hungry!

There is no time to worry because
the silence is shattered by a loud roar.

Being very agile,
Archie quickly
runs to the top
of a nearby tree.
Just in time!
A dangerous-looking tiger
has come searching
for a meal. She does
not see him.

When he is sure it is safe, Archie climbs down the tree with some coconuts for breakfast.

He LOVES coconuts!

Next, Archie sets out to build a house. Fortunately, he finds many things he can use on the beach.

driftwood

hammer

strong vines

thorns for nails →

saw

The coconut grove is a perfect place. He is a hard worker.

First, he puts in the floor.

For walls, Archie uses palm leaves because they let in a bit of breeze.

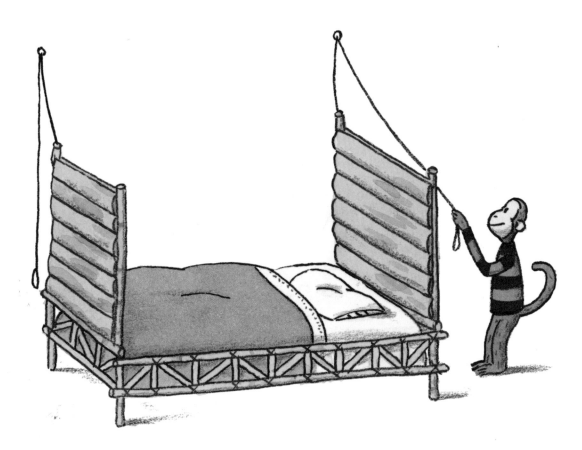

He builds a comfortable bed,

which is also a breakfast table.

Archie finishes just in time. An inquisitive ibis
named Clarice has been watching his progress.
She stops in and says, "Hello."

Clarice keeps Archie company
as he sits on his new porch.

Archie loves games, so he makes a checkerboard
and teaches Clarice to play.

Later, Clarice teaches Archie to fish.
"How peaceful!" says Archie.

One morning,
while collecting wood,
Archie does not notice
the tiger right behind him.
There is no escape.

He bravely prepares to meet his end.

The tiger
regards Archie
for quite some time—
then . . .

. . . she gives him a big wet tiger kiss! She thinks
Archie is very brave, and his sweater reminds her
of her cubs. The tiger, Beatrice, has been very lonely
since her cubs grew up and moved away, and she is
glad to have a new friend.

They decide to have a party
to celebrate their new friendship.
Clarice helps with the decorations.

Archie cooks his specialty:
fish and coconut soup. They
have a wonderful meal, with
fried bananas for dessert.

"My favorite!"
says Beatrice.

After dinner, there are rides and entertainment. Archie plays his flute and Clarice sings. She has a beautiful voice.

That night, Archie crawls into bed and drifts off to sleep. It has been a perfect day.

In the morning, Archie is jolted awake with terrible news. Rough and smelly pirates have landed on the island and captured Beatrice!

"HAR," the pirates say,
as they taunt her cruelly.

What to do?!! It seems hopeless.
What *can* they do?
"We must remain calm," says Clarice.

Good advice! Archie pulls himself together.
Soon they have come up with a plan. It
involves catapults, which Archie has designed.

By noon, they have built two of them, hidden near the pirates' camp. Clarice and her bird friends fill the baskets with slimy, rotten fruit.

Then Archie paints fierce monkey faces on all his coconuts. They finish as night falls, just in time!

At the pirate camp, Captain Pequod
has set First Mate LaFaargh to keep watch
while they sleep, partly because he likes saying
his name (LA FAAAARGH!), but mainly
because LaFaargh has trouble sleeping.
Clarice and Archie watch and wait.

Now Clarice sings her
most soothing lullaby,
so softly and sweetly
that even First Mate
LaFaargh falls fast asleep.

"Shhhh," says Archie, as he
and Clarice quietly free Beatrice.

They put the
coconut heads all around
the pirate camp.

By morning, all is ready.
As the pirates wake up, they
see the tiger has escaped!
In her place is a note:

When Archie gives the signal, the catapults are
released. Tons of rotten, squishy, smelly mangoes, kiwis,
papayas, and bananas (Beatrice's favorite) rain down
on the confused pirates.

Everywhere they look, they see fierce monkey faces.
"Shiver me timbers!" cries Captain Pequod.
Beatrice roars her scariest roar.
It is too much for them.

They flee, never to return,
carrying First Mate LaFaargh,
who is still fast asleep.

All the island
creatures join the
three friends in a
tremendous cheer:
"HOORAY!"

Archie climbs to the top of a tall tree. "Thank you, my new friends," he says. "We make a good team. Why don't we become neighbors? We can help one another build houses in this beautiful spot."

Everyone thinks this is a fine idea.

And it was.